Tangled

Read-and-Sing

DISNEP PRESS

New York • Los Angeles

For information address Disney Press, 1101 Flower Street, Glendale, California 91201.

ISBN 978-1-4847-0843-9
F383-2370-2-14122
Printed in China
First Edition
1 3 5 7 9 10 8 6 4 2

For more Disney Press fun visit www.disneybooks.com

Contents

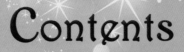

Tangled

Once upon a time, in a faraway land, a drop of sunlight fell to the ground. The drop grew into a magical golden flower that possessed healing powers.

An old woman named Mother Gothel discovered the flower. Mother Gothel was vain and wished to be young forever. And so she kept the flower hidden.

Centuries passed, and a glorious kingdom was built close to the cliff where the flower grew. When the kingdom's beloved queen fell ill, the townspeople searched for the legendary flower. At last they found it. The flower made the Queen well, and she soon gave birth to a beautiful baby girl with magical golden hair.

One night, the vengeful Mother Gothel slipped into the nursery and cut off a lock of the baby's hair. But the hair lost its power and turned brown. Mother Gothel knew that if she wanted to stay young, she had to keep the child with her always. She snatched the princess and vanished to a place where no one could find them.

Mother Gothel named the girl Rapunzel. She locked her in a soaring tower and raised her as a daughter. Though the woman pretended to love Rapunzel, she only truly loved Rapunzel's golden hair.

Rapunzel kept herself very busy. She was happy with the companionship of Mother Gothel and her friend Pascal, a chameleon. But she had one dream that she longed to make come true.

On the day before her eighteenth birthday, Rapunzel told
Mother Gothel her wish. "I want to see the floating lights!"
she said, revealing a painting she had made of them. "They
appear every year on my birthday—only on my birthday. And
I can't help but feel like they're meant for me!"

But Mother Gothel told Rapunzel she was too weak and
helpless to handle the outside world. "Don't ever ask to leave
this tower again," she said.

Meanwhile, in another part of the forest, a thief named Flynn Rider was on the run with his partners in crime, the Stabbington brothers. Flynn held tightly to a satchel that held a stolen royal crown!

Flynn knew the Stabbingtons were too dangerous to be trusted, so he left them and took off with the satchel. But the captain of the guard and his horse, Maximus, were hot on his heels!

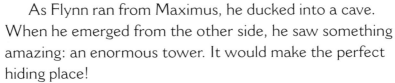

As Flynn ran from Maximus, he ducked into a cave. When he emerged from the other side, he saw something amazing: an enormous tower. It would make the perfect hiding place!

Flynn climbed the tower and scrambled through the open window at the top. Finally, he breathed a sigh of relief. He was safe!

CLANG!

Suddenly, everything went black.

Flynn had found Rapunzel's tower.

The girl was so startled by the intruder that she hit him with a frying pan.

Rapunzel dragged Flynn to the closet and stuffed him inside. She felt exhilarated! Surely this act of bravery would prove to Mother Gothel that she could handle herself in the outside world.

Then Rapunzel noticed the mysterious gold object in Flynn's satchel.

She placed it on top of her head and gazed into the mirror. She felt different somehow.

Suddenly, Mother Gothel arrived home. Rapunzel began to ask her again about the floating lights, but Mother Gothel cut her off.

"We're done talking about this!" she yelled. "You are not leaving this tower! EVER!"

Rapunzel realized she would never see the lights if she didn't take matters into her own hands. So she asked Mother Gothel to get her a special paint for her birthday. She knew the request would take Mother Gothel away from the tower for three full days.

Mother Gothel left, and Rapunzel dragged Flynn out of the closet. She told Flynn that if he took her to see the floating lights and returned her home safely, she would give him the satchel. Flynn had no choice but to agree.

As much as Rapunzel longed to leave the tower, when the moment came, she was terrified. She had never been outside before.

With Pascal on her shoulder, she slid down her hair, stopping just inches above the ground. Slowly, Rapunzel touched one foot to the soft grass, then the other.

"I can't believe I did this!" she shouted as she rolled on the ground.

Soon she and Flynn were on their way.

Not far from the tower, Mother Gothel came face-to-face with Maximus.

"A palace horse," she gasped, seeing the royal crest. She thought the guards had found Rapunzel, and raced frantically back to the tower.

Mother Gothel searched everywhere, but Rapunzel was gone. Then she saw something beneath the staircase. It was the crown and Flynn's WANTED poster.

Flynn, meanwhile, had led Rapunzel to a cozy-looking pub called the Snuggly Duckling. Inside, the place was filled with scary-looking thugs!

Suddenly, someone recognized Flynn. The thugs decided to turn him in for the reward money.

Rapunzel banged her frying pan on a giant pot to get the thugs' attention. She asked them to let Flynn go so that she could make her dream come true.

To Rapunzel's surprise, every one of the thugs had a secret dream, too.

Suddenly, Maximus and the royal guards burst into the pub. "Where's Rider?" demanded the captain.

But Rapunzel had won over the thugs, and one of them showed her and Flynn a secret passage out of the pub.

They were not safe for long. Moments later, Maximus led the guards straight to the escape route.

Maximus chased Flynn and Rapunzel to the edge of an enormous cavern. Rapunzel lassoed her hair around a rock and jumped! She swung over the wide ditch and landed on a stone column.

Meanwhile, Flynn fended off Maximus and the guards with Rapunzel's frying pan! Rapunzel tossed her hair to him and held on tight as Flynn swung through the air!

But they still weren't safe. A dam suddenly burst, filling the entire cavern with water! Maximus and the guards were washed away, and Flynn and Rapunzel were trapped in a small, dark cave.

The water quickly began to rise. As Flynn frantically searched for a way out, he cut his hand on a rock.

"It's pitch black. I can't see anything," Flynn said.

"This is all my fault," Rapunzel said tearfully. "I'm so sorry, Flynn."

"Eugene. My real name's Eugene Fitzherbert," Flynn admitted. "Someone might as well know."

"I have magic hair that glows when I sing," Rapunzel admitted.

Suddenly, Rapunzel realized that her hair could light up the cave and show them the way out!

At the tunnel's exit, Mother Gothel waited for Flynn and Rapunzel, but the Stabbington brothers emerged instead. She offered them revenge on Flynn—and something even more valuable than the crown.

Meanwhile, Rapunzel, Flynn, and Pascal had made it safely to shore. Rapunzel wrapped her hair around Flynn's injured hand and began to sing. Her hair glowed and healed Flynn's wound. Flynn was dumbfounded. He was finally beginning to understand how truly special Rapunzel was.

When Flynn went off to gather firewood, Mother Gothel emerged from the woods to take Rapunzel back to the tower.

But Rapunzel refused to go back. "I met someone, and I think he likes me," she said.

Mother Gothel laughed at her. She handed Rapunzel the satchel with the crown and told her that it was all Flynn wanted.

Rapunzel wanted to trust Flynn but she wasn't sure. She decided to hide the satchel in a nearby tree.

The next morning, Flynn woke up to Maximus trying to drag him away!

Rapunzel came to Flynn's rescue and talked the horse into letting the thief go free for one more day.

As Flynn and Maximus shook on their truce, a bell rang in the distance. Rapunzel ran toward it until she came to the crest of a hill. Rapunzel gasped as the entire kingdom came into view. Her dream was just hours away from coming true!

Rapunzel, Flynn, Maximus, and Pascal entered the gates of the kingdom. The town was the most exciting thing Rapunzel had ever experienced. As a group of little girls braided Rapunzel's locks, Rapunzel's eye fell on a mosaic behind the stage. It was of the King and Queen holding a baby girl with striking green eyes, just like her own.

As evening approached, Flynn led Rapunzel to a boat and rowed them to a spot with a perfect view of the kingdom.

Watching the lanterns fill the sky, Rapunzel's heart soared. She decided to give Flynn the satchel. She was no longer afraid he would leave her once he had the crown.

Beneath the glow of the lanterns, Rapunzel and Flynn held hands and gazed into each other's eyes.

Suddenly, Flynn spotted the Stabbington brothers watching them from the shore. He quickly rowed the boat to land.

Flynn tried to give the brothers the crown, but they wanted Rapunzel! Knocking Flynn out, they tied him to the mast of a boat and set him sailing into the harbor, the stolen crown on his lap. Then they came for Rapunzel. Luckily, Mother Gothel saved her.

Seeing Flynn rowing away without her, Rapunzel agreed to go home.

Back at the tower, Rapunzel sat in her bedroom, heartbroken. As she looked at her paintings, she realized suddenly that she had been painting the kingdom's flower symbol her whole life. Then she thought about the princess's eyes. That was when she knew: *she* was the lost princess!

Rapunzel confronted Mother Gothel, who admitted everything.

Meanwhile, Flynn had been captured with the crown and been arrested. But he had escaped to rescue Rapunzel from her tower.

"Rapunzel! Rapunzel, let down your hair!" he called.

Rapunzel's golden locks fell to the ground.

When Flynn reached the top of the tower, he found Rapunzel chained in the middle of the room. He went to help her, but Mother Gothel wounded him with a dagger and chained him to the wall.

Rapunzel was desperate to save Flynn. She begged
Mother Gothel to allow her to heal him. In return, Rapunzel
promised Mother Gothel she would stay with her forever.

Mother Gothel agreed to the deal and unchained
Rapunzel.

But Flynn would not let Rapunzel sacrifice her freedom.
Grabbing a shard of broken glass off the floor, he cut off
her hair! It instantly turned brown and lost its magic healing
power.

"What have you done?!" Mother Gothel cried. Within
moments she aged a hundred years and turned to dust.

Rapunzel cradled Flynn in her arms and began to weep. A single golden tear fell upon Flynn's cheek. To Rapunzel's astonishment, the tear—and then Flynn's entire body— began to glow.

Rapunzel had saved Flynn. It was time to go home. . . .

Rapunzel's Challenge

Rapunzel happily skipped through the forest. All her life, she had dreamed of visiting the palace. And now, with Flynn as her guide, Rapunzel had finally left her tower and was on her way there!

Flynn, on the other hand, was not so happy. He was supposed to be running *away* from the kingdom. But how could he change Rapunzel's mind?

Suddenly, Flynn had an idea. "You know, Blondie," he said, "the forest can be dangerous. It's no place for someone like you."

Rapunzel frowned. "What do you mean 'someone like me'?" she asked. "Anything you can do, I can do, too. In fact, I'll bet that I can do it better than you!"

"Did you say 'bet'?" Flynn grinned. "Well, why don't we have a contest to see if that's true? If I win, I get back my satchel and you promise to go home."

Rapunzel shook her head. "No, the satchel can't be part of the bet. The prize should be something else." She thought for a moment. What could the winner get? Then she looked at her chameleon friend, Pascal. He rubbed his tiny green tummy eagerly.

"Oh, I know!" Rapunzel exclaimed. She pulled out her frying pan and pointed it at Flynn. "Whoever loses has to make the winner a snack."

"You're on, Blondie," Flynn said. He looked around and then pointed to a nearby tree. "You think you can beat me to the top of that tree?"

Rapunzel squared her shoulders. In a flash, she threw her long hair onto a low branch and swung gracefully up into the tree.

"Hang on!" Flynn cried, dashing after her. "I didn't say go!" He quickly pulled out two arrows and used them to climb up the tree, right past Rapunzel.

When he'd almost reached the top of the tree, Flynn
stopped and looked down. Rapunzel was nowhere in sight.
"She's an even slower climber than I thought!" Flynn
mumbled to himself.

Suddenly, from up above, he heard a voice call down.
"Yoo-hoo! Flynn Rider! What took you so long?"

Flynn looked up and gasped. Rapunzel was sitting on the top branch of the tree. "How did you get up there so fast?" he cried.

Rapunzel pointed proudly to her golden hair. "You'd be surprised how much I can do with this," she said. "No branch is too high for my hair to reach."

"That's cheating," Flynn argued. "You can't use your hair to help you. I demand another contest. And this time, no hair."

Rapunzel happily agreed. This time she picked the contest. "How about a race?" she said.

Flynn nodded. "First one to the river wins," he said.

Pascal gave the signal, and then they were off!

Rapunzel and Flynn sprang forward from the starting line. It wasn't long before Flynn took the lead.

But as he raced along, Flynn noticed a WANTED sign tacked to a tree. His picture was on it! But the nose looked slightly off. . . .

"Not again!" Flynn moaned. The WANTED posters always showed him with a fat, crooked nose.

Flynn was staring so hard at the poster that Rapunzel sped right past him. Her gleaming hair trailed behind her.

I can't lose! Flynn thought. He doubled his speed . . . and accidentally tripped over Rapunzel's hair! Before he knew it, he was completely tangled in her long locks.

When Rapunzel reached the river, she turned around. To her surprise, she saw Flynn wrapped up in her hair.

"That wasn't fair," he panted. "You used your hair again."

"No, I didn't," Rapunzel argued. "I only used my legs."

Rapunzel sighed. It seemed they would need one more contest!

Flynn pointed to the wide river in front of them. "Let's see who can cross this first," he said.

Uh-oh, thought Rapunzel. How could she win *this* one? She didn't know how to swim!

As Flynn dove into the water, Rapunzel looked around. "Any ideas?" she asked Pascal, who was hanging from a nearby vine. The little chameleon shrugged. But then Rapunzel's eyes lit up. "That's it!" she cried.

Flynn panted as he climbed out of the river. He was dripping wet. "I did it," he said happily. "I won!" Then he looked up, and his jaw dropped.

Rapunzel was standing on the shore, as dry as she had been on the other side.

"I don't understand," Flynn sputtered. "You got here first? And you're not even wet?"

Rapunzel nodded. "That's because I didn't swim across," she said. "I swung across."

Flynn grinned slyly. "Then I win! Remember? We made a deal that you couldn't use your hair."

"I didn't use my hair," Rapunzel said. She held up a long, thick vine. It stretched all the way back to a tall tree on the opposite side of the river. "I might have learned how to swing on my hair," she explained. "But this time, I used this!"

Rapunzel chuckled at the thought of Flynn swimming through the river as she swung right past him.

Flynn sighed. He hated to admit it, but Rapunzel had
beaten him. Again. Glumly, he poured the river water
out of his boots. "Fine, you win." He sighed. "Come on,
Blondie. It's on to the kingdom now, I guess."

"Wait. What about the prize?" Rapunzel reminded him.
She pulled out her frying pan. "You owe us a snack. And
we're hungry! Aren't we, Pascal?"

"Well, what would you like?" Flynn asked Rapunzel.

"Surprise us!" Rapunzel answered excitedly.

While she and Pascal waited in the cool shade of a cherry tree, Flynn built a fire. Then he began to gather nuts and cherries and cook them.

"Mmm!" Rapunzel said a few moments later. It was one of the tastiest treats she'd ever had.

"You know," Rapunzel told Flynn with a wink, "you might be almost as good at cooking as I am . . . almost."

Rapunzel's Forest Friends

Rapunzel and Flynn were on their way to see the kingdom's floating lights. Rapunzel could not stop looking at the world around her. After she had been stuck in her tower for so many years, everything was a discovery—from the tallest tree to the tiniest pebble. Rapunzel wanted to learn about all of it! She stopped to smell some flowers and picked a few more to add to her bouquet.

"These are so beautiful!" she exclaimed. "What are they called—AAAAAAH!"

A branch in the bushes had started to move—only it wasn't a branch. It was a pair of antlers. And the animal with the antlers was now staring at Rapunzel! She stumbled backward, tripped over her flowing hair, and fell down.

Rapunzel scrambled to her feet and hid behind Flynn. "It's just a deer," he said. Then a smaller creature with long ears hopped out of the bushes. "What is that?!" she cried.

"Hey, whoa, easy," Flynn said. "Okay, I can see you haven't been introduced. Rapunzel, meet the fiercest animal in the forest: a wittle bunny wabbit."

A whole family of bunnies hopped out of the bushes and began playing together. Rapunzel peeked at them from behind Flynn.

"You're telling me that a tough cookie like you is afraid of a couple of fuzzballs?" Flynn asked over his shoulder.

Rapunzel didn't want Flynn to think she was afraid. So she slowly made her way closer to the bunnies and knelt down on the grass. They seemed just as curious about her as she was about them. Soon she was surrounded by new furry friends.

A chipmunk scurried out of his hole and birds flew over to join the little group. Before long, Rapunzel and the animals were playing a game of hide-and-seek.

"This is the most fun I've had in . . . forever!" she told them. Rapunzel had only been out of her tower a short while, and she was already having the time of her life!

But someone else wasn't having any fun. Flynn tapped his foot impatiently. "So if playtime is just about over," he said, "maybe we could move on? Mosey along? Get going? What do you say?"

"Come on!" Rapunzel called to Flynn. "Don't just stand there. Go hide! It's my turn to count."

Flynn laughed at the idea. "Uh, no. I don't do games," he said.

The animals wanted Flynn to play, too. The birds and the chipmunk brought over some leaves and twigs to help him get started on a hiding place.

"Hey! Quit it!" Flynn cried, shooing them away.

Then the bunnies and the deer tried to help. If Flynn wasn't going to build a hiding place, maybe they could build one *for* him.

But the animals had trouble covering him completely! And there was definitely no hiding the scowl on Flynn's face.

"Never mind," Rapunzel said to her friends. "I guess he really doesn't want to play." And with that, she led the animals away for another round of games.

Rapunzel called back to Flynn, "If you change your mind, we'll be over here, having a wonderful time!"

But Rapunzel didn't stay away for long.

Minutes later, she hurried back to show Flynn the new animal she'd found.

"Oh, my goodness!" Rapunzel cried as she burst out of the bushes. "Look at this cute guy. I had no idea bunnies could grow so big!"

"That's no bunny!" shouted Flynn.

"Then what is he?" Rapunzel asked.

"BEAR!" Flynn yelled. Then he spotted the bear cub's mama. "I mean, TWO BEARS!"

In a panic, Flynn turned and scrambled up a tree. Rapunzel watched from below with her two new friends. She didn't understand how Flynn could be afraid of such adorable animals.

"Oh, great! *Now* you're hiding!" Rapunzel teased. "I guess you *do* want to play with us after all!"

Flynn sighed. If Rapunzel could get over her fear of bunnies, maybe he could be friends with a bear. He turned his back to Rapunzel and started climbing down the tree.

"All right, fine. I'll play," he said as his feet hit the ground. "You'll see, I'm excellent at hiding."

He turned. Rapunzel was gone. So were the animals.

"I'm sure you are," came Rapunzel's voice from the bushes. "But you'll have to find us first!"

A Day to
Remember

apunzel could hardly believe it. In just a few hours, she was going to see the floating lights. Now she looked around the village, her eyes filled with wonder.

"Look how many stores there are!" Rapunzel said to Flynn. She ran along sidewalks decorated with royal purple flags and past clerks selling their wares. "There's a pastry store, a clothing store, and . . . oh!"

Rapunzel raced across the street and pushed her nose against a window. "A whole store for books!"

As Rapunzel turned away from the window, a vegetable seller stopped her. "How about some nice carrots for your horse?" he said.

"Oh, thank you!" Rapunzel said, taking a carrot and giving it to Maximus. Then she skipped on down the street.

"Ahem." The vegetable seller coughed and held out his hand. Flynn grinned slyly and shook his head. Rapunzel sure had a lot to learn!

Flynn paid the vegetable seller and then raced to catch up with Rapunzel—before she could get into any more trouble!

By the time Flynn caught up to Rapunzel, she had walked into an art studio and was talking to a painter.

"Oh, Flynn. This is Roberto," she said. "Aren't his paintings beautiful?"

"Ah, Flynn," Roberto said. "Are you an artist as well?"

Flynn laughed. "Me, an artist?" He dragged Rapunzel over to a mirror. "Look at this face. It is meant to *be* painted! Although they never get the nose quite right. . . ."

Rapunzel rolled her eyes. She was about to say something back to Flynn when Roberto interrupted her.

"Perhaps you would like an art lesson?" he offered.

Rapunzel could hardly believe her ears. She was so excited she couldn't even speak. She just stood there with her mouth hanging open.

"That's a yes," Flynn said.

"Well, then, we have no time to waste," Roberto said.

"An art lesson from a real artist," Rapunzel said with a smile. "Flynn, can you think of anything more perfect?"

Flynn was half asleep in Roberto's chair, his hair flopped over his eyes. Pascal stuck out his tongue, zapping Flynn on the nose.

Flynn jolted awake. "I heard you," he snapped. "I'm just trying to get a little beauty rest before my portrait."

The chameleon flared his nostrils. Didn't Flynn know that Rapunzel was going to paint Pascal? After all, he'd been her best friend for years. He hadn't just come on the scene . . . like *some* people.

Rapunzel laughed at her friends. "We'll see what I feel like painting once we get started."

Pascal didn't like the sound of that. He had to show Rapunzel what a great subject he was. He hopped from one of Roberto's paintings to another, blending in with each one.

"Okay, Pascal. You are a master of color." She picked him up. "And a master of disguise! Now let's get going."

Rapunzel shoved Roberto's supplies into Flynn's arms and pushed him out the door. "Oh, Flynn," she said, "isn't this exciting? And it's all thanks to you. If you hadn't come into my tower, none of this would be happening."

Soon the group reached the meadow. Roberto set up his supplies and Rapunzel began to paint a landscape scene.

"Good, good," Roberto said encouragingly. "Perhaps some shadowing here. Pay attention to how the light is hitting over there."

"Oh, thank you," said Rapunzel. "I see now. Flynn, what do you think?"

But Flynn and Pascal had fallen asleep.

Rapunzel chuckled and crept over to the two. Bending down, she leaned over Flynn and shouted, "WAKE UP!"

Flynn jumped into the air. "How about that portrait?" Rapunzel said.

Flynn grinned. It was about time. He settled on a rock and began to pose.

"The hardest stroke is always the first one," Roberto said. He took his handkerchief out and patted his forehead. "You need to capture the moment for the portrait to be truly great."

Rapunzel studied Flynn for so long that he fell asleep again.

With Roberto's help, Rapunzel worked to capture the scene. Finally, she was finished. When Flynn saw it, he could not help laughing. He had a fly sitting on his nose, and his mouth was hanging open.

"What do you think, Pascal?" Rapunzel asked. "Pascal?"

Rapunzel looked around. Pascal was nowhere to be found. She searched under the bushes and near the river, but still there was no Pascal.

Rapunzel's eyes began to tear up. The floating lights would be rising soon. Seeing them without Pascal wouldn't be nearly as special.

"He must be here somewhere," Flynn said, checking under a bush. But all he found was a scared squirrel.

"Rapunzel, I don't think your frog wants us to find him," Roberto said.

"He's a chameleon," Rapunzel said. "And he's my best friend." She sniffed a little and put her head in her hands. "He must be very angry at me for something. . . ." Her voice trailed off as she started to sob.

Suddenly, there was some rustling in the bush behind Rapunzel. In a flash, a pale green Pascal leaped out of the shrub. He landed right in Rapunzel's lap.

"Where'd you go, Pascal?" Rapunzel asked. "What's wrong? Were you jealous because I was painting Flynn?" She stroked Pascal's head. "Silly chameleon, you have no reason to worry. You're my best friend."

"I hate to break up this lovefest, Blondie," Flynn said, "but we'd better get back to town if we're going to see those lights."

Back in town, Roberto put Rapunzel's paintings on display. He was just admiring a painting of Maximus when a woman walked in.

"Oh, this horse is perfect," the woman said, looking at the painting. She backed up from the portrait and tilted her head. "The brushstrokes are wonderful, and I love the choice of colors for the background. Why, he almost looks as if he could step right off the canvas!"

As the woman admired the
painting, a cat jumped out of her
bag. Spotting Pascal, the cat gave chase.
Up and down the shop the two ran, knocking
over paintings.

"I'm so sorry," the woman said when she caught her cat.
Then she looked back at the horse painting. "This really would
look lovely in my home," she said. "How much?"

Rapunzel couldn't believe it. She had just sold her first
painting. Like a real artist!

Later, as Flynn and Rapunzel set out to see the lights, Flynn looked at Rapunzel and smirked. "Race you to the water," he said.

Rapunzel smiled slyly. "You're on!" she said. Then she surprised Flynn by jumping on Maximus and racing away.

Flynn raced behind her. He was sure this wouldn't be the last time Rapunzel surprised him!

The Jewels
of the Crown

Rapunzel was excited! She had defeated Mother Gothel and saved Flynn's life. Now she and her friends were on their way back to the kingdom. Soon she would meet her true parents, the King and Queen.

"I can't believe I'm the lost princess," said Rapunzel. "I don't know how to be a princess."

Flynn smiled and said, "You'll be great as a princess. All you have to do is wear a huge, heavy crown. . . ."

"Oh, my!" Rapunzel exclaimed. "Though of course it's not a requirement," Flynn added quickly.

"Let me start over," Flynn said. "Do you remember that tiara from my satchel? Well, let me tell you a story about that.

"When I was a kid in the orphanage, I read a book about the princess and her tiara. The book said this tiara symbolized everything the princess should be.

"The tiara's white crystals stood for a strong, adventurous spirit; green represented gentleness and kindness; red stood for courage; and the round golden crown itself stood for leadership.

"For years, I thought of that tiara, and then one day, I actually met a gal who could wear it. She certainly was adventurous.

"As she traveled toward her dream, she also showed kindness toward everyone, courage, and definitely leadership. She just seemed able to turn every bad situation into something wonderful!"

"Flynn, are you talking about—?" Rapunzel started.

"You!" Flynn exclaimed. "I'm talking about all those amazing things you did when you left your tower in search of those floating lights."

"But I did all those things when I had long, magical hair!" Rapunzel exclaimed. "Now I can hardly stand up straight. I feel off balance. I have no idea how to help anyone without magic."

Suddenly Flynn and Rapunzel heard
a commotion behind them.
"Nobody move!" someone shouted.
Several men emerged from the trees,
ready to attack! "Just hand over your
horse!"

Flynn leaped into action, chasing the thieves. "Rapunzel!"
he shouted. "Run away, and don't look back!"

But Rapunzel did not run away. She ran right into the middle of the fray, trying to rescue Maximus.

Flynn leaped onto Maximus's back. But the horse accidentally bucked Flynn off as he fought against the thieves.

When it was over, Rapunzel scolded the bandits.

"It's all my fault," one man replied. "I need your horse to take my son to the doctor."

"Oh, my! Where is he?" Rapunzel asked.

Within minutes, Rapunzel was tending to the boy's injuries. He smiled in relief as he was hoisted onto Maximus for a ride to the kingdom's doctor.

"How can you ever forgive
us?" the men asked Rapunzel.

Rapunzel thought of the
tiara—adventure, kindness,
courage, and leadership.
Suddenly, she realized she
didn't need her magical hair.

"Come with me," she said.

At the palace, Rapunzel received her princess crown. As she waved to the crowds, she knew that no one was as supportive as her faithful new friends! And they always would be, too.

Rapunzel's Royal Wedding

Flynn and Rapunzel had been back in the kingdom for months. Rapunzel was happily getting to know her parents again and was growing even closer with Flynn.

Now spring had sprung, and Flynn had a surprise for Rapunzel. Max kept guard, and Pascal went along to play. But Flynn wanted to be alone with his princess.

As dusk fell, Flynn took his chance to
jump into a boat with Rapunzel. The lovely
night reminded them of times past.

Flynn wanted to propose! He put his hand in his pocket, but— oops! He did need Pascal and Max, after all. They had the ring!

"Will you marry me?" Flynn finally asked Rapunzel.

"Yes," Rapunzel said sweetly.

Rapunzel couldn't wait
to tell everyone the happy
news. On the way home,
she and Flynn stopped at
the Snuggly Duckling.

Rapunzel's friends were delighted. They
had been waiting for news of this wedding!

Of course, Atilla helped Rapunzel design a cake.

They baked and iced, but nothing seemed quite right.

But with some extra hard work, Rapunzel
and Atilla finally created the wedding cake of
her dreams!

Of course, there were floral arrangements.

But it took Tor and a field of wildflowers to please Rapunzel!

As for ring bearers, the choice was clear: Maximus
and Pascal could not have been prouder to accept!

When it came time to find a dress,
Rapunzel was determined to design her
own. She sketched and sketched. . . . But
she simply could not make up her mind!

The pub thugs tried to help, but their dresses didn't seem right either.

Luckily, the Queen arrived. "Darling," she said. "I want to help you find the perfect dress." And she did!

On the morning of the wedding, bells rang throughout the kingdom. Everyone was excited to see the King and Queen happily riding in the royal coach.

Max and Pascal were thrilled—until Max sneezed. The rings flew into the air!

As the friends raced to retrieve the lost rings, the King proudly took Rapunzel's arm.

Flynn beamed when he saw Rapunzel.
Inside, everything was perfect. But outside,
Max and Pascal were on a mission. . . .

In fact, Max and Pascal were wreaking havoc on the kingdom.

Max chased one ring . . . .

. . . and Pascal chased the other.

Everything was almost perfect . . . until they crashed into the tar factory.

Still, Max and Pascal returned to the wedding just in time for the exchange of the rings—despite their wild adventure and odd appearance.

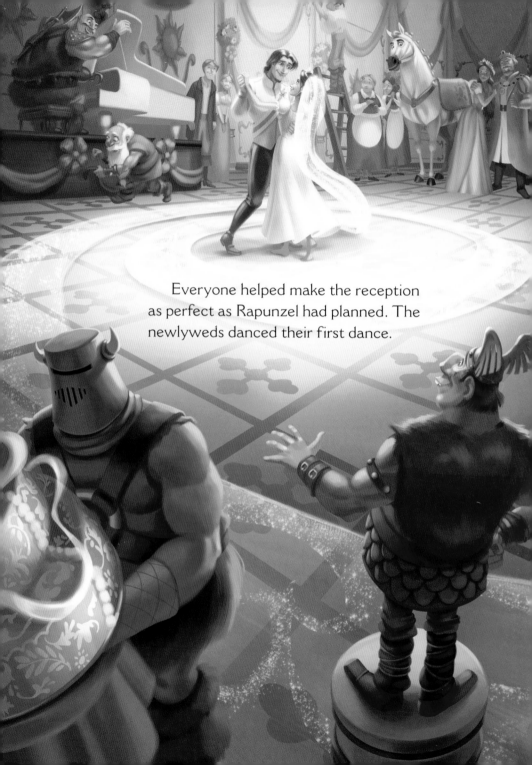

Everyone helped make the reception
as perfect as Rapunzel had planned. The
newlyweds danced their first dance.